To

From

Who udderly loves you!

Inspired by Holly Reagan

With thanks to Jane Horne and Claire Page

Copyright © 2007

make believe ideas

27 Castle Street, Berkhamsted, Hertfordshire, HP4 2DW.

Manufactured in China

I udderly love you!

Kate Toms

make
believe
ideas

sque-e-e-eze!

sque-e-e-eze!

I love
everything about you:

Your tail, your ears, your toes.

I love the softness
of your skin,

your silky, s-moo-th, wet nose.

I love your every moo-vement,

8

the way you skip about,

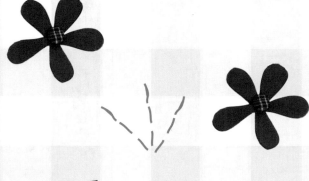

and how your **hooves** point inwards,

while all your

knees

stick out!

I love the way
you chatter,
the funny things you say,
the **moo**-sic
that you sing to me,

the silly games we play.

13

And when you go exploring,

tweet! tweet! tweet!

DOG

it makes me really proud,

Grrr!
Grrr!

to know you'll always find me,

even in a crowd.

At nighttime, in the **moo**-nlight, when the stars shine overhead,

I watch you as you're sleeping in your snuggly, little bed.

zzzZZZZZZZZZZZZZ

ha-ha!
ha-ha!

I love you when you're happy,

I love you when you're sad. Moo-hoo!

Even when you're **moo**-dy, not meaning to be bad.

It's great to be your mommy,
I love you
through and through,

I UDDERLY, UDDERLY LOVE YOU

and I know you love me too!